About the Book

Mole and Troll, friends who don't pull any punches, are up to their old antics in four new heart-warming stories.

As usual, they are busy teasing and pleasing each other. Who else but two good buddies would fight to see which one can balance a mushroom on his head the longest? And who else but best friend Troll would assure a worried Mole that he does not have to dress up in fancy clothes and say funny things to be appreciated?

Tony Johnston and Cyndy Szekeres team up once more to depict the pranks and tender moments found in a solid friendship.

A See and Read Storybook

HAPPY BIRTHDAY, MOLE & TROLL

BY TONY JOHNSTON
DRAWINGS BY CYNDY SZEKERES

G. P. PUTNAM'S SONS   NEW YORK

For Walter

Text copyright © 1979 by Tony Johnston
Illustrations copyright © 1979 by Cyndy Szekeres
All rights reserved. Published simultaneously
in Canada by Longman Canada Limited, Toronto.
PRINTED IN THE UNITED STATES OF AMERICA

LIBRARY OF CONGRESS CATALOGING IN PUBLICATION DATA
Johnston, Tony.
Happy birthday, Mole and Troll.
(See and read storybook)
SUMMARY: Mole and Troll learn several lessons
about friendship in these four stories.
[1. Friendship—Fiction. 2. Birthdays—Fiction.
3. Short stories] I. Szekeres, Cyndy. II. Title.
PZ7.J6478Hap [E] 78-25717
ISBN 0-399-61137-1

CONTENTS

CONTESTS

Flowers were blooming.

The stream was bubbling.

The sun was bright.

"Hello, spring," said Troll.

"Hello, stream. I feel so good,

I bet I can skip this little stone

twenty-seven times."

Mole came along. He felt good too.

"I bet I can skip this little stone

twenty-eight times," he said.

"We will see about that," said Troll.

Troll stood back.

He took some
running steps.

He skipped his little stone.

One, two, three, *plop*,

went the stone across the water.

Then Mole stood back.

He took some running steps.

One, two, three, *shplop*,

went the stone across the water.

"I was just warming up," said Troll.

"Me too," said Mole.

"I had a kink in my skipping arm."

"I am tired of skipping stones

anyway," said Troll. "Let's see

who can count the most ants on a leaf."

"Fine," said Mole.

Troll saw some ants carrying things
across a leaf. He started counting.
"One, two, three, four, five . . ."
"What are you counting?" asked Mole.
"There are no ants on that leaf."
"Fifteen, sixteen, seventeen . . ."
"Troll, there are no ants here!"
shouted Mole, peering at the leaf.
"Thirty, thirty-one, thirty-two . . ."

"Stop counting! That is nothing but
a big green leaf with NO ANTS!"
"There are exactly ninety trillion,
nine hundred ninety-nine
million ants carrying things
on that leaf," said Troll.

"There is not one single, stupid ant
on that leaf !" shouted Mole.
"Then you cannot see at all!" yelled Troll.
"Right," said Mole. "Moles have bad eyes.
Let's do something else." "Fine," said Troll.
But he did not feel fine. He felt mad.

"Let's see who can balance a mushroom
on his head the longest," said Mole.
"I am good at that."
"Okay," said Troll.
"But you better watch out, Mole,
because I am great at that."

Mole chose a good mushroom for balancing.

He put it on his head.

Troll chose a good mushroom for balancing.

He put it on his head.

They walked everywhere, trying to keep

their mushrooms on their heads.

Then, *boff*, they walked into each other.
"You did that on purpose
to knock my mushroom off!" yelled Mole.
"My mushroom would have stayed
up there forever!"
"You bumped into me
because I was
winning!"
Troll yelled
back.

"My mushroom was steady as a rock!"

Mole and Troll were angry.

"Okay," said Troll.

"This is the last contest.

This will show who is best

once and for all.

We will see
who can hold his breath the longest."
"I can do that for an hour," said Mole.
Troll took out a big stopwatch.
Mole and Troll watched
the little hand go round and round.
Then Troll
shouted,
"Go!"

They held their breath for dear life.
They got red in the face.
They got purple in the face.
They got blue in the face.
And—WHEEEEE!—
out came all their breath
like a train whistle.

"Mole," said Troll.

"Yes, Troll?"

"I feel bad."

"Well, I feel worse."

"Stop that," said Troll.

"It doesn't matter who is best."

"Right. It doesn't matter since
I can beat you at everything.
We are still friends."
"Mole," said Troll, "are you fooling me?"
"Yes, I am," said Mole.

DRAGON FIRE

It was a gray afternoon.

Thick clouds hung low in the sky.

Mole and Troll did not care.

They were cozy beside the fire.

Then—FLASH!

A bright glow lit up the sky.

"Dear me!" squeaked Mole, jumping up.

"What was that big flash?"

Troll was about to say something when—

BOOM!

A big noise followed right after the flash.

Troll crouched on the floor
with his hands over his ears, shouting,
"Hide me! Hide me!"
But Mole could not do that.
He was hiding himself.
FLASH! BOOM!

Mole sat on top of Troll
because he was too scared
to do anything else.
He cried, "My grandfather warned me
about flashes and booms!"
"He did?" asked Troll.
"Yes, he did."
FLASH! BOOM! FLASH! BOOM!

"What is it?" cried Troll.

"I can't remember," moaned Mole.

"Please try," screeched Troll.

Mole thought about everything

his grandfather had ever told him

(which was a lot).

FLASH! BOOM! FLASH!

BOOM! A-BOOM!

Leaves shivered and shook on the trees.

The house shivered and shook.

Mole and Troll shivered and shook

and hugged each other tight.

By and by Mole cried out, "Dear me!"

"What is wrong?" asked Troll.

"I remember what flashes and booms are."

"Tell me. Quick!" shouted Troll.
"They are Dragon Fire!" yelled Mole.
Troll hid under the sofa pillows and
screamed,
"Don't tell me
any more!"

But Mole could not stop talking.
"A fierce dragon is spitting
fireballs at us—
like a big green cannon—
and rumbling down from the hills."
FLASH! BOOM! FLASH!
BOOM-BA-BOOM!
The Dragon Fire went on and on.

Mole and Troll hugged each other till
they almost squeezed their breath away.
Then there was silence.
Mole and Troll listened.
They heard something
thumpeting down hard
on the roof like angry fingers.
"Rain!" cried Troll.
"Rain!" cried Mole.
And he added,
"Dear me!"
"What is wrong now?" asked Troll.
"I am," said Mole. "Flashes and booms
are not Dragon Fire.

They are lightning and thunder.

They come with the rain.

Grandfather told me all about them.

He *liked* them."

"Well, I don't," said Troll.

"They scare my breath away," said Mole.

"But they keep my very best friend
right next to me. And I like that."

"You are right," giggled Troll.

FLASH! BOOM!

One more flash came. And one more boom.

Nobody jumped.

"Did that scare you?" asked Mole.

"No," said Troll. "Did that scare you?"

"No. Flashes and booms are not scary

when you know what they really are."

"Mole?" asked Troll.

"Yes, Troll?"

"Who thought of the dragon?"

"I did," said Mole proudly.

"You have a wonderful imagination."

"Thank you."

"But please keep it to yourself,"
grumbled Troll.
"Oh, Troll." Mole laughed.
"Oh, Mole." Troll laughed.
Then they settled down to enjoy the fire
in the quiet that follows a storm.

THE NEW MOLE

Mole was in his attic.

He was thinking.

He thought, "Troll knows me too well.

He never notices me.

I am like a rock. Or a weed.

Or a dirty dish.

I am just one of the pile.

I am a boring friend."

Mole felt low.

He looked in an old trunk.
He found some fancy clothes
and put them on.
He strutted by the mirror.

"Wonderful!" cried Mole.
"I have fancy clothes.
I will say funny things.
I will be a brand new mole.
Troll will not believe it!"

Troll dropped in.

"Mole!" he called. "Where are you?"

"Toodle-oo, Old Trolly! Just
hustle on up," chirped Mole.

"Here is jolly old Mole."

Troll came up.

He looked in the attic.

He did not believe it.

"Hi-ya, Trolly," said Mole.

"Uh—hello, Mole."

"Just call me Moley," sang Mole.

"Er—thanks."

"Well, sit yourself down," twittered Mole.

"I am going to tell some jokes."

Troll was glad to sit down.

He felt weak.

"Ready?"
cried Mole.

"I guess so," said Troll.

"Why did the mole cross the road?"

"I don't know," said Troll.

"To get to the other side!
Har! Har! Har!"

Mole laughed loudly at his own joke.

Troll did not laugh.

"Didn't get it, huh?" said Mole.

"Here's another.

Why did the mole tiptoe past
the bedroom door?

So's not to wake the sleeping bag!"

Mole slapped his knees and howled
till he cried.

Troll did not laugh.

He got up to go.

"Sit yourself down, roly-poly Trolly.

I will recite a poem."

Troll sat down.

Mole recited. He recited. And recited.

"Stop!" cried Troll.

"No. This is too much fun!"

"No it isn't. I am going home."

"What is wrong?"

"I miss my dear old Mole. Where is he?"

"That wet blanket?" shouted Mole.

"He is a plain, fuzzy, gray,
silly, very boring mole!"

"Yes," said Troll sadly.

"I miss him because he is just
plain, fuzzy, gray, silly, boring—
and lovable."

Mole felt silly.

He rushed behind a screen.
He took off his fancy clothes.
He stuffed them in the trunk
and stepped out quietly.
"Here I am," he said.
"Mole!" cried Troll. "Oh, Mole!
Where are those awful clothes?"

"In the trunk," said Mole.

"I am saving them for Halloween."

"Good," said Troll.

Then they just sat quietly

on top of the trunk

and talked together.

And they liked it.

HAPPY BIRTHDAY

One day Troll woke up excited.

"Mole!" he shouted. "Come up!"

Mole came up.

"What is it?" he asked.

"Do you know what day it is?" asked Troll.

"Tuesday," said Mole.

"I mean what *day* it is?" said Troll.

"Well, Troll, when you say it like that,
I don't know."

"Are you sure?" asked Troll.

"I am sure."

"Guess what day it is, Mole.

It is one of your favorite days."

"Christmas!" shouted Mole.

"It is Christmas! Where is my present?"

"It is not Christmas. Guess again."

"Halloween. Boo!" cried Mole.

"It is not Halloween either," said Troll.

"I will give you a hint."

"Good," said Mole. "A hint will help."

"It is somebody's birthday," said Troll.

That was a good hint.

It was such a good hint,

Mole knew whose birthday it was.

"Goodbye, Troll," he said quickly.

"See you later."

Mole hurried home.

He rustled in his desk.

He found scissors, paper, doilies, ink, pencils, paste, and sequins.

He went to work.

Then he bustled in the kitchen.
He found flour, sugar, baking powder,
eggs, milk, vanilla, and chocolate.
And he went to work.

In a little while, Mole called Troll.

"I am ready," he called.

"Ready for what?" asked Troll.

"For a surprise. Come and see."

Troll liked surprises. He came to see.

"Happy Birthday, Troll!" shouted Mole,

grinning from ear to ear.

Troll was really surprised.

"Thank you, Mole," he said.

"Now I have a surprise for you."

"What?"

"It is not my birthday."

Mole stared at Troll.

"It isn't?"

"No," said Troll, patting him gently.

"Oh," groaned Mole. "How dumb of me."

"You are not dumb. You are kind.
Who else would give me a party
when it is not my birthday?"

"Troll?" asked Mole,

"whose birthday is it?"

"That is the best surprise of all.

It is *your* birthday!"

Mole sat down.

"Well, isn't that nice," he muttered.

"It is my birthday.

It is MY BIRTHDAY!" he yelled.

Troll laughed.

"Wait right here," he said.

"I will," said Mole. "I am too surprised to move."

Knock. Knock. Knock.

Mole opened the door.

There was Troll with a

big birthday cake.

"Happy Birthday, Mole!" he said,

grinning from ear to ear.

"Oh, thank you, Troll!"

"You are welcome, Mole."

Then Mole said, "Wait right here."

He ran to the kitchen
and came back with a big cake too.
"Happy Birthday, Troll!" he said.
"But it is *your* birthday," said Troll.
"I want to share it with you," said Mole.
Then they each made a wish
and blew the candles out.

About the Author

Tony Johnston grew up in California and attended the University of California at Berkeley and Stanford University, where she got a master's degree in education. She taught elementary school and worked in publishing before moving to Mexico City with her husband. They have two little girls, Jennifer and Samantha. Ms. Johnston is the author of THE ADVENTURES OF MOLE AND TROLL, MOLE AND TROLL TRIM THE TREE, THE FIG TALE, NIGHT NOISES AND OTHER MOLE & TROLL STORIES, LITTLE MOUSE NIBBLING, FOUR SCARY STORIES, ODD JOBS and FIVE LITTLE FOXES AND THE SNOW.

About the Artist

Cyndy Szekeres grew up in Fairfield, Connecticut, and studied art at Pratt Institute in Brooklyn. She now lives in Putney, Vermont, with her two sons, Marc and Chris, and her husband, artist Gennaro Prozzo.

She is the illustrator of NIGHT NOISES AND OTHER MOLE AND TROLL STORIES and FIVE LITTLE FOXES AND THE SNOW.